Books for Boys

Rocket Ship

By

My books are a project to get my son to enjoy reading. The stories use early reading words and subject matter young boys like. The words in the book range from pre-primer through third grade words. Early readers will find reading and learning more enjoyable because of the appropriate and interesting content.

For all boys who find reading boring!

Making Reading Fun!

© 2013 Marc Sevigny. All rights reserved.
ISBN 978-1-304-08649-5

Rocket Ship

"I am tired of this video game. There is nothing to do. This is the worst day ever!"

My mom calls me to the kitchen. She asks me to help cover the food and wash the bowls. "Hey, this gives me a great idea."

I put the bowls and tin foil into a big box. I take the box up to my tree house.

My friends like to play rocket ship, so I will make one we can play in. I will put on a little paint here and there, and look, I made a rocket ship!

5, 4, 3, 2, 1,

BLAST OFF

Red fire came out of the bottom of my rocket.

My rocket ship started to go up. I said, "This is so cool!"

I had to set the speed and push the right buttons.

"Wow!" I am in outer space.
I turned to look behind me
and could see Earth.

I looked out my window and could see some very big stars. I had to turn my rocket quickly to miss a few planets.

A voice on the radio said "Get your spacesuit on." I put on the spacesuit and was ready.

I jumped out and was floating in space. "This is so cool!"

I want to go walking on the moon. I slowly go down. My friends will not believe I was on the moon. I will put a flag in the dust to show I was here.

"Away I go!" This is such a
fun adventure. "Look!"
There is Earth. I think I can
see my tree house.

It is funny what you can do with a box and a little imagination.

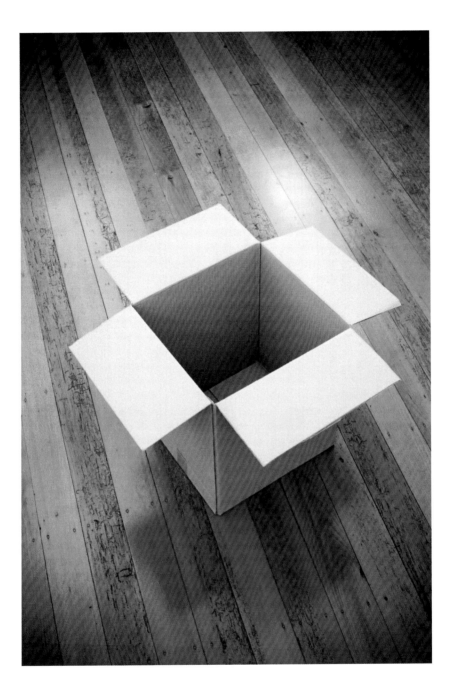

The End

Keep Reading!

More Books from Mr. 7 Yea!

The Hunter
Cowboy
Fire Fighter
Runaway Sailboat
Cool Forts
The Fish that Ate Me
Lost Campers
Baseball Wars
Dinosaurs